Black Noise

edited by Ayesha Kinley
and Abigail Brookes

LIKE THIS PRESS

Cover image by Ayesha Kinley and Abigail Brookes.

ISBN: 978-1-909506-17-6

First published by Like This Press in 2017.

LIKE THIS PRESS
https://likethispress.wordpress.com/

Black Noise

CONTENTS

Black Noise is a concept we wanted to apply to both literary and visual art. Inspired by the turbulence of twenty first century events, and the ignorance of the everyday. We envisioned a book built on black humour, melancholy, absurdity and the uncanny, merging to create both invasive and emotive portrayals of modern life.

- *Abigail Brookes & Ayesha Kinley*

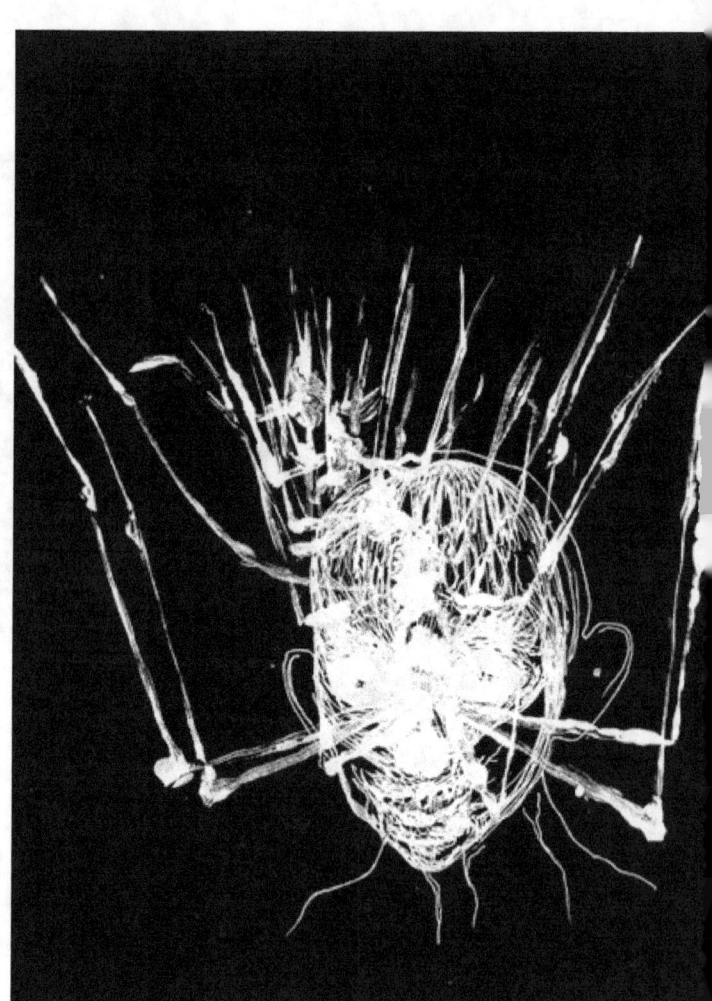

THE COFFIN SHOP
David Cook

'So the deluxe model, then... lightweight, durable, lovely silk lining, gorgeous deep varnish finish, Wi-Fi, plenty of leg room...'

'Wi-Fi?' said Charles. 'Why... why would it need Wi-Fi?'

The salesman, known by his name badge as 'Jamie J – Coffin Genius', eyed Charles. 'Charlie,' he said. 'Can I call you Charlie?'

'I'd rather you didn't,' stammered Charles. 'Charlie,' continued Jamie. 'You've gotta have Wi-Fi in your coffin these days. Your dad, right, I bet he loved his mobile phone, right?'

'Not really, he could only just about turn it on.'

'Everyone loves their mobiles, course they do,' said Jamie. 'So we're finding that more and more of our clients – actually, we think of them more as *friends* than clients, friends we're meeting just that little bit late – want to have their phones buried with them.

'Now,' he continued, words cascading over Charles' attempts to interrupt. 'Sure, you could get the basic package,' – said with a sneer and a condescending look – 'with its polyester lining and no way for your dad to Tweet from the grave...'

Charles' eyes boggled.

'...but you want the best for your old man, right Charlie?' He patted Charles' on the back, making him wince.

'But I really don't think...' said Charles weakly.

'Look Charlie,' said Jamie, all slicked back hair and shark-like grin, 'My old dad, he's coming to the end of his time, right, and he said to me, 'Jamie,' he said, 'I want the best. I don't want to be uncomfy down there, you know me, I like my creature comforts. And I'm a tall man, Jamie, so I need lots of leg room. And worse,' and you know Charlie, I almost shed a tear at this bit, 'and worse, I can't be without YouTube. You know how I love my videos of cats falling off tables. What am I going to do six feet under without that? I'll be bored off my nut.'

'So I said, 'Dad, come down to the shop with me. We'll pick you out something fancy, and I'll keep it for you for when you go.' And he did, and he chose not the deluxe, but the *super-deluxe* model – complete with Netflix subscription, Sky TV, massage cushions and a mini-fridge stocked with beer, the things they do these days - and what's more, I said, 'Dad, seeing as it's you, I'll give you a three per cent discount.' And he gave me such a big hug, and he kept telling me how much he loves me, what a brilliant son I am, I could barely shut him up. I mean, you've gotta do the best for your old pops, isn't that right? I know you agree with me, Charlie.'

By this point, Charles was simply nodding along.

'Tell you what, Charlie,' said Jamie, putting his arm around Charles. 'I wouldn't normally do this, but let me take you into the back, and I'll show you the coffin I've got reserved for my dad. It's the business. I'll do you a deal on one just like it.'

He guided Charles through the showroom, past a display of discount coffins ('Buy one, get two free!') at the back and through some double doors. Down a corridor, and into another room.

'There,' said Jamie. 'Isn't she beautiful?'

It was, Charles could just about recognise through his mental fug, an exceptional looking coffin. It was twice the size of any he'd ever seen, with burnished brass handles, plump purple cushions and crafted from deep, varnished inviting oak. Inside, it had a little television screen, a small fridge, and a phone charging socket. It radiated luxury, and almost made you wish you were dead so you could have a go in it without feeling awkward.

Jamie circled his prey. 'And what's more, Charlie, seeing as it's you, I'll give you a five per cent discount. That's even more than I gave to my old man, but I think you and me are on the same wavelength, you know what I mean?'

Charles gulped. 'How much is it?' he squeaked.

'Thirteen thousand, seven hundred and fifty pounds?!' screeched Charles' son Martin, studying the bill a couple of days after Gramps had been laid to rest. 'For a *coffin?* Dad, have you gone completely bloody mad?!'

'It's got Wi-Fi in it,' said Charles. 'And Netflix.'

'Netflix! *Netflix!* Gramps only just about worked out that there was a Channel 5 last year, and you think now he's dead his corpse is suddenly going to wake up and start watching Breaking Bad?! He's *dead,* Dad, he doesn't need Wi-Fi!'

'He can Tweet, the man in the shop said. And watch YouTube. And all that.'

'What? Is he going to emerge at the Pearly gates, phone in hand and send us Snapchat pictures of the angels? Or does he just lie in the coffin for the rest of eternity, watching YouTube videos while his limbs rot off?'

'I'll remind you that this is your Gramps you're talking about. Don't be so disrespectful. The man said sometimes corpses do really just 'wake up' as you put it, and need some entertainment.'

'Look, sorry Dad, but… *jeez*. When did Gramps get a phone that could do all that anyway?'

'I bought one for him, through the Coffin Shop. Look, it's toward the bottom of the bill.' He pointed at numbers. 'I put it in your Gramps' suit pocket during the viewing. Only forty-five quid a month, unlimited calls and texts, 20 gig of data, the man said it was a good deal.'

Martin's face was as cold as his grandad's corpse. 'I'm going down to that bloody shop,' he said icily, '*right now* and I'm going to tell them—'

He was interrupted by a short buzzing noise from his pocket. He had a tweet.

'Hi buddy – 1st tweet! Coffin v comfy – & loving Breaking Bad. #Fab! Bit lonely tho, follow me back! Luv, Gramps. X x'

Martin looked at his phone, looked at his dad, and fainted.

EITHER WAY, IT'S GOODBYE
Nick Ryle Wright

One too many wrong turns and this is where you end up. Saturday evening and you're hanging around outside the disabled toilets in a crumbling mall in a town you've come to hate. There's a dull pain in your groin and the cheap clown outfit you're wearing – stained in more than one place with your own blood – has earned you the suspicion of the young mothers standing protectively in front of their children over by the food court. They're discussing you and your dubious intentions with the thin, shaven-headed security guard who, to your jaundiced eyes, looks even more suspect than you.

Maybe they just don't buy it, the bucket full of change, the balloons and the stickers. Perhaps they think you're some kind of shyster who's not, in fact, working on behalf of St. Anthony's Children's Hospice. It's a cynical world, but what are you going to do about it? Exactly. Time to shift your thoughts back to the suicide you'll never get around to. Noose, pills, or human fireball? Too many options.

The toilet door creaks open and your morbidly obese partner Morris – dressed in a much larger, though otherwise identical costume to your own – appears by your side. Your head fills with questions you don't want to ask.

'Sorry,' Morris whimpers. 'Sometimes there's no stopping it.'

The security guard asks to see some form of identification. You oblige. He's shocked to see that you're legit. It surprises you too, sometimes. Behind him, the two mothers direct inaudible obscenities at you. You give them the finger and then you leave, one hour before you're supposed to. This is it, you tell Morris. You're done with this life.

Outside, a strip of orange sky sits above the office blocks. Light gleams off the windows. You feel woozy, stumble into a lamppost.

Morris asks: 'Would you like Julia Roberts to make you better?'

You tell him no.

'But she was a nurse, back in her own country.'

It's a kind offer, but again, you decline.

'Hey, I know! Why don't you come back for some food? Julia was the best cook in her village.' Morris is a good person – better than you – but there's a mounting list of dampening truths you'd like to tell him about this world of ours.

You sneeze out the blood that's been congealing in your nostrils all day. The last twenty-four hours are a bit of a blur, but at some point, possibly whilst Morris was juggling plastic eggs for that fat toddler with the sty, you popped a pill. Several bars later, you washed up at the greyhound track where you proceeded to gamble away the day's takings. There was a fight. For reasons you can no longer remember, you came to the defence of a grey-haired man in a smart suit who later bought you drinks and paid women to dance for you at an out-of-town strip club. You remember his back-of-the-throat laugh, how he said you were the first clown he'd ever seen throw a punch. He congratulated you on your technique, said he admired any man who was prepared to take a beating for a stranger. He told you he ran a big organisation up north, that he had plenty of work for a man like you. He gave you his card, told you to come up and see him sometime. You look at the card now, ready to accept his vague offer, terms unknown.

'I'm calling you an ambulance,' Morris says, his huge fingers urgently punching the keys on his ancient mobile.

You shoot him a look. You know from bitter experience that there's nothing worse than being a clown in A&E on a Saturday night. Besides, today is your cousin Dale's twenty-first birthday and you've heard that his parents are throwing him a party at the Sundown Club. You won't be welcome, but you still plan to make an appearance. It's been five years since the accident and there's no way you're going to leave town without finally saying sorry; without saying goodbye.

You give your collection box to Morris. It will be safe with him. He'll take it to the charity's office and all will be well. Good things will be done with the money. Bets will not be laid. You shake his clammy hand, hoping that whoever takes your place treats him well. You hope that Julia Roberts sticks around for a couple more months. You hope, but you're not hopeful.

Back at your one room basement flat, you notice that the door is ajar. Cautiously, you step inside. You pick up the distinctive aroma of your landlord, Goldthwaite: sulphur and TCP with a hint of cigar smoke. The place is a mess. Drawers and cupboards have been opened; your clothes have been cut to shreds and stacked in a messy pile on the floor; your bed sheets have been defecated on.

You call his name.

No answer. The mice move behind the cooker. The tap drips.

Last week the two of you nearly came to blows when he let himself into the flat at 3 a.m. and threw a bucket of cold water over you as you slept. Bile bubbling in his throat, he ordered you to cough up all the rent money still owed to him. You told him you didn't have the funds and probably never would have the funds and that you were planning to denounce him as a slum landlord. Hissing like a cornered snake, he quoted a few passages from the Bible before informing you that you were going to hell. *Tell me something I don't know*, you said, before mocking his newly-acquired faith, telling him that no amount of prayer and flagellation would ever succeed in making him any less terrible.

You catch sight of yourself in the mirror. You're in a bad way: grey skin and dark eyes with a growing paunch. Your ribs begin to ache. You may have forgotten last night's blows, but your body has not.

Lifting up a section of loose floorboard at the end of your bed, you feel around inside the cavity until you find your grandfather's pocket watch, left to you, his eldest grandchild, in his will. Very carefully, you peel back the layers of cream-coloured paper just to check that Goldthwaite hasn't swapped it with a Timex. It's a minor miracle the thing is still in your possession, that you haven't already pawned it. You open it up and observe the still hands. Shame creeps up on you. You wrap it back up, tuck it into your pocket and leave. There's nothing else worth saving.

The coach station is busy. Everyone wants to leave this place. The ticket machine isn't working. You want to punch a hole in the screen, hurl abuse at it as though it was a sentient being, but you don't, because you're being stared at; clown or no clown, there's just something about you that engenders mistrust. Against your will, you'll have to speak to the plump woman with the tiny nose, beckoning you towards her window. You forget where you're heading, so you check the card. It's a town you've never heard of. You hope your new job, whatever it may be, involves driving; transporting unknown contrabands from one remote shithole to another. You can handle that. You are not a people person. You crave the solitary life.

The woman hands you the ticket. Your coach leaves at nine.

You head north out of town, towards the Sundown Club. Birds chirp incessantly as you tramp along the grass verge with all the inexactness of a drunk. You could tumble into the ditch or step out in front of a lorry and no hearts would break.

Resting for a while beside a wooden fence, you look out into a field, speckled with rooks. You remember the dark silhouette of your grandfather, emerging through the mist, his dogs either side of him as he returned from his morning inspection of the upper fields. He was the proudest man you ever knew. What would he say if he could see you now? He'd tell you that you've lost your way, that you have a head full of good ideas that are going to waste. He'd be wrong.

Moving through the Sundown Club's glass-fronted reception, you feel as conspicuous as you look. An artificially bronzed receptionist watches you closely before reaching for her phone. *There's just something about you.*

You follow the arrowed signs to the conference room. Once there, you take a moment to survey the gathered faces, some as familiar as your own, others less so. People have aged, grown wider, become greyer; cousins you remember as children are now adults. And then you see Dale, sitting in his wheelchair beside a table stacked high with still-wrapped gifts. He looks happy, but this is what you *want* to think. You want to imagine that his is a life worth living.

The club's waiting staff provide you with welcome cover as you make your way towards your cousin, now sharing a joke with three attractive women, each hanging on his every word. No woman has ever listened to you the way they're listening to him. You like the look of the brunette with the thick eyebrows and the ankle chain, but there's no time to entertain thoughts like that.

Dale seems surprised to see you. No wonder. He looks up at you like he's trying to work out the punch line to a bad joke. His companions step back, alarmed and disgusted.

You scan the room. So far, no one's clocked you, which is surprising, seeing as how you're a beaten-up, bloodstained clown.

You ask Dale how he is. A stupid question, really. On the night of his sixteenth birthday, you allowed him to get high and drink himself stupid at your impromptu house party. At some point in the early hours, you presented him with the keys to your van. Take it for a spin, you said, wanting some time alone with Vicky Finch. Thirty minutes later, your van was resting on its roof at the bottom of a steep embankment. When he woke from his medically-induced coma, Dale told everyone that he'd taken your keys without asking. Nobody really believed him. You tried to visit him in hospital, and later at the rehabilitation centre, but each time you were turned away by angry relatives who made it clear that you were no longer one of them.

'I can't believe it,' Dale says, his eyes reddening.

You stare at his unmoving hands, fixed to the arms of his chair. There's almost a decade between you but you always thought of him as a brother.

Dale laughs. Seconds later, he starts to cry, but he can't wipe away his own tears. He looks off to his left, like he knows trouble is imminent. 'Does anyone know you're here?'

'Look, I just wanted to say –'

'No. Please don't. Don't say it.'

But you do.

Dale smiles as you lay your hand on top of his. You can see in his eyes that there's a lot he'd like to ask you, but this isn't the moment to dump your sorry tale on him. You won't tell him about how you quit university before graduating; about the succession of shitty jobs that followed; about the women who wouldn't stay. And neither will you explain how a counsellor once suggested you might've deliberately sabotaged your own life as an expression of your remorse for ruining Dale's. You won't say these things. Instead, you say:

'I'm leaving tonight. For good. I just wanted you to know.' You hear angry voices – a commotion. You place the pocket watch on Dale's lap. 'And I want you to have this.'

'What is it?'

'Something I don't deserve.'

A heavy hand lands on your shoulder. This is it.

'Out! Now!' Dale's brother Jack twists your arm behind your back and pushes you out into the middle of the room. Now everyone's watching. You spot your mother and father standing together by the window. For a second or two you have their attention, but then they turn away, like you're not there.

'What the fuck?'

You recognise your sister's voice.

'What the fuck is this piece of shit doing here?'

You say her name: 'Fay!'

'Don't fucking talk to me.'

Fay helps Jack to steer you outside. Together, they push you down the steps. Your knee turns awkwardly and you land heavily on your back.

'Fucking prick.'

There's a distant roll of thunder. You close your eyes and await the rain.

Noose, pills, or human fireball? Too many options.

Your coach leaves at nine.

Either way, it's goodbye.

NO SECOND NIGHT OUT
Thomas McColl

The No Second Night Out initiative to tackle the problem of homelessness was definitely working, though not in a way that anyone at the outset could ever have envisaged. One thing was for sure; it was no longer being directed by the Mayor. Someone – or something – else was now in control.

At any rate, when Outreach worker Jan rang Flo at the Centre for the fourth time that night, it was yet again to report that there was no-one at the scene. In this case, an elderly man they knew called Bill who always slept beneath an aluminium awning in a dimly-lit alleyway directly behind a small road of shops and cafes, just a couple of blocks away from Oxford Street.

'…There's this strange smell as well, not a smell from the bins but something much worse.'

Jan had put her phone on speaker so that Tim, her colleague out with her tonight, could listen in on the conversation too. Like Jan, he was wearing a zipped-up jacket. Even though it was the middle of summer, the temperature today had dipped considerably, and already tonight was much colder than this time last night, with the weekend set to get even colder.

Jan couldn't imagine what it was like to sleep rough each night in the summer, let alone winter, yet that was what poor old Bill had been doing for months each night at this spot, and before that, over many years, at various other spots in central London. Though he was one of the entrenched homeless – who'd resisted every attempt by Outreach to get him into an emergency shelter (let alone any kind of temporary or permanent accommodation) – it was imperative Bill was worked on just as much as new arrivals.

Jan remembered last week when Bill complained about her waking him up each night. She'd been trying her best to explain to him that Outreach were now much more pro-actively trying to get people off the streets and into shelter, but as soon as she said it was part of this new initiative, No Second Night Out, he cut her off.

'No second night out?' he growled. 'Well, I'm way beyond that. My first night out was years ago. And so, you're far too late. Why can't you just leave me alone?'

He had a point, but even if he wanted to be left in peace, the guys from Outreach weren't going to give up. The first-nighters would, of course, be the easiest ones to convince and therefore help, but no-one was to be left behind, not even Bill.

Tonight, however, for the first time since the initiative started, Bill was missing, and yet he'd been here, for his distinctive red and orange sleeping bag was left behind, albeit ripped to shreds as if by a crazed wild animal...

...which was a similar scene to what Jan and Tim had found already at all three of the other locations they'd been to as a result of calls the Centre had received that night from members of the public – though until they saw Bill's torn up bedding, both volunteers had started to wonder if some idiot was playing a prank.

'Well, it can't be some tasteless joke if Bill's bag is ripped up too,' said Jan, holding the phone near her chin while Tim stood beside her with his ear cocked. 'Clearly, something's seriously wrong, like some kind of extreme violence has happened. It's as if Bill was suddenly attacked in his sleep then taken away.'

'I know, it's so bizarre,' replied Flo, her voice crackly but audible. 'Abdul called just minutes before you and said the same thing; that so far him and Dean have found only ripped up sleeping bags as well.'

'We've scoured the whole alleyway twice,' said Tim. 'Checked everywhere, but Bill's definitely gone.'

'Well, I've rung the police,' said Flo. 'And they've sent a car to Waterloo, where the five discarded sleeping bags were found. I've asked

Emily and Stuart to wait there beneath the bridge until they arrive.'

'And what do you want me and Tim to do?' asked Jan.

Flo began to speak but something flew into Jan's face and, thrown off balance, she dropped the phone, which smashed into pieces on the ground.

'Shit!' gasped Jan, as Tim shooed the insect away with his hand.

'Moths!' he growled, and Jan, looking up, saw there were now three moths swirling around them.

It was like the tiny creatures had been attracted to the light of the screen on the phone, but as soon as it smashed they flew off and took to swirling around what had now become the nearest source of light, a wall-mounted lamp above a graffiti-covered metal-shuttered entrance, and though the light had been working fine when Jan and Tim arrived, it was now flickering intermittently.

'There were moths at the other three places we went to as well,' said Tim, as he helped Jan pick up what remained of her phone.

Jan paused for a moment to digest this information. 'You're right, there were,' she said, frowning.

Tim glanced down at the sleeping bag they were both stood at the edge of, then looked about him nervously.

'We need to get out of here,' he said, his voice slightly shaky but still calm. 'I've no idea what Flo was going to tell us to do, but there's no good reason for us to hang round here any longer. This is for the police to deal with.'

Tim got out his phone and, cupping it with his left hand to shield the light from the moths, searched for the telephone number of the Centre, while Jan, taking a step back, looked down at the spot where Bill had been sleeping last night and remembered the usual brief exchange of words they'd had.

'Are you alright, Bill?' she'd ask, crouching down beside him. He was wrapped up even more tightly than usual in his sleeping bag, as if he was in some kind of cocoon, with only part of his face – his mouth and the bottom of his nose – barely visible.

'Yes, thanks. I'm dead alright.'

'I'm dead alright.' That was always his answer, his low gravelly voice, as ever, sounding tired and vexed.

'Are you warm enough there?'

'Yeah.'

'You don't want to go indoors?'

'No.'

'No? OK.'

So that was that. There was nothing more that Jan, Tim or anyone else from Outreach could do. If Bill said no, then they had no choice but to leave him where they found him – though no matter how many times he'd refused (and even if he'd been seeing all these nightly visits as low-level harassment), two people from Outreach had always returned the following night to ask him again.

As Jan herself said in an on-message piece to camera for BBC London News just weeks before:

'...We never give up. It might take weeks, months, even years, but we'll always be there, chipping away, and sooner or later, one way or another, we'll get a result, and the next step – a run-in shelter – is just the start of a journey in getting someone off the streets and into accommodation...'

In reality, though, what Jan was actually starting to feel about her work was decidedly off-message. The Mayor, when he launched the No Second Night Out initiative, announced that *'by the end of this year, no-one will live on the streets of London, and no individual arriving on the streets will spend a second night out'...*

...but it surely wasn't a coincidence that this measure had been quickly introduced just as the worst recession in years was starting to bite.

Instead of No Second Night Out, thought Jan, it should be no cuts to benefits, wages and services. Maybe then there wouldn't be such a huge rise in the number of people ending up homeless. But then, with the Government hell bent on cutting the deficit whatever the human cost, it was unlikely that the problem of homelessness was going to be solved in London any time soon. Already, there'd been a 25% increase in the number of people sleeping rough in the last year alone, but on the other hand, as a direct result of No Second Night Out, 83% of them didn't return for a second night on the streets. So more people sleeping on the streets but spending less time there: What did that mean? That things were getting better or had actually got much worse?

Jan had been moaning to Tim about it.

'I hate the way they describe benefit cuts as 'benefit changes',' she said, talking about a Government announcement that day.

'I know,' said Tim, sighing, but sounding slightly bored at having to talk about this subject for the umpteenth time that night.

'It's never a change for the better, is it?'

'You're right about that.'

However, all talk of benefit cuts had been replaced by talk of serrated cuts – the weird slashes in Bill's bedding.

Tim had given up trying to get through to Flo – the line was constantly engaged – but decided that, before leaving the alleyway, he'd use his phone instead to take a photo of the sleeping bag and, prepared this time for the moths already circling around him, had it gripped firmly in his hands.

'What could have done this?' he asked, as he took a close-up shot of the slashed material.

The smell that Jan had described to Flo was getting worse, much worse.

'C'mon, Tim, let's go,' said Jan, feeling on edge. She thought she heard a sound from behind the nearest bins – two large round metal ones. She investigated but, peering round the back of the bins, found nothing there.

Then she heard Tim's phone smash on the ground and looking round, was stunned to see him with his legs suspended off the ground, and the whole of his head being gorged on by a hideous creature with a huge distended mouth, massive globular eyes, and an exoskeletal frame that was as hard and grey as the concrete it was stood upon, as if it had literally risen up out of the ground.

Jan screamed, and the creature looked her way. Its distended mouth began to retract, with Tim's head still inside it, within seconds it had closed completely. Tim's headless body fell to the ground, the neck a bloody stump. Jan closed her eyes for a second, then opened them again, but the creature was still there. She couldn't believe what she was seeing. This thing, though roughly human-sized, was implacably insect: Even what had looked, a moment ago, like an ankle-length cape was actually a pair of wings which now splitting, revealed a pulsating abdomen and thorax, and three pairs of scaly, tubular, jointed limbs. Its mouth, no longer enlarged, was the only part of its face that actually looked human, but then, as it opened up again, a pair of barbed mandibles shot out, and Jan gasped as the creature, with its shoulders hunched, awkwardly loped towards her. Totally horrified, she couldn't move from where she was stood between the two metal bins, transfixed by the sight of this humanoid insect with a bristle-lined leathery face that despite the globular eyes and mandibles, and translucent membranes instead of ears, had this human mouth that looked strangely familiar.

As she backed, stumbling, further into the space between the two metal bins, Jan realised why: The mouth was Bill's. Harassed Bill – whose voice was now inside her head ('I'm dead alright') – was looming over her, engulfing her in shadow as she often did when standing over him. Feeling the brick wall behind her, and realising now there was no escape, she slid down onto the ground, curled up into a ball and closed her eyes. She could only pray it'd be over quickly.

Morrisons

Morrisons Supermarkets plc BD3 7DL
Kirkstall - 0132 422804
VAT No.343475355

TY DESCRIPTION	PRICE	AMOUNT
1 M REUSABLE BAG	.10	£0.10 A
1 M DIPS	£1.00	£1.00 D
1 M MOROCCAN HOUMOUS	£1.00	£1.00 F
1 FREEDOM KITCH TOWEL		
1 RADISH	000000031010	
1 M COURGETTE	VISADEBIT	
1 M Cott	: ************8993	
1 Dat	: 0414	

```
ue Number       : 00
a Source        : ICC
chant Number    : 2536480
minal ID        : 27875529
nsaction        : 596691
horisation      11 - 0833
. Date          117
ified / PIN
      CHANGE                    £0.00
      Number of items:             15
```

MULTISAVE £0.2
SAVINGS AT MORRISONS
****
Today you would save earns 25 po..t

Our Match & More Terms and Conditions have changed
For more details visit www.morrisons.com
****

Sainsbury's

live well for less

LEE...

Sainsbury's Supermarkets Ltd
33 Holborn London ...
www.sainsburys.co.uk
VAT NUMBER: 660 45... 36

THINK 25   Cashier confirmed ... r 8
 *TTS SOAVE CLASSICO
 *TWO INDIA PALE ALE
 * 2 500... LAGER
BM../BER... CONC...
POMODORINO TOMS   £1...
J. WHITE COUS GRATE   £1... 0
S. CHOC MSSE X6   £1...
S. LMN/GNGER FS...   £...
J. OLIVES GAR 250...   £2...
S. IN. AGUR   £2...
S. TNBKD MARG P...A   £1.8
S. TNBKD MARG P...A   £1.8

BALANCE DUE   £24.
Visa Debit   £24.
...CC ********** ***** 7043
...TE. 031010
...AN SEQUENCE. ...
MERCHANT ... **69106
...TH CODE... 055914

SMOKE
Ian Seed

I bumped into Gerald R. near the centre of Turin, just outside the college where I was working. He had kept his long hair and beard, though they were now matted and streaked with white. Shouting to make myself heard above the traffic, I asked after his wife (whose name I couldn't remember) and daughter, Laura. He said she was being treated for depression, but I didn't know whether he was referring to his wife or daughter. The latter I remembered as a lively and curious toddler. The Italian doctors weren't much use when it came to mental illness, he told me, taking the cigarette I offered and sucking furiously as if that were now the most important thing in the world.

It struck me just how long we had been living abroad. I was only here by chance. I had met Gerald in a bar years before when I was on my way to the station after a backpacking tour. It was he who had told me about the college job. Somewhere I still had my unused return train ticket to England. I wondered absurdly if it might still be valid.

I felt a soft punch on my shoulder. Gerald wanted to know if I could spare him another cigarette.

PLASTIC
Andrew Ballantyne

My thoughts have been merciless since you left. I always find time to dwell on the three and a half years that we spent discovering one another in our early twenties. There was a version of yourself that was not obscured by judgement and expectation and I found it. Teased from your exquisite subtleties where it once blushed behind colder facades; I found it. It will always remind me of a time when I could feel something.

'We're here, Mr Sutcliff,' the taxi driver's voice instantly snapped me out of my daydream.

I tried to capture a closer look at my destination but the house itself was guarded by a row of towering evergreen trees, broken only by the iron gates that offered entry onto the winding driveway.

'Thank you, driver. I appreciate it's a little out of the way.' He nodded apprehensively. We were sat at the bottom of a natural pit where the surrounding hills met. I stepped out of the car and watched it fade away into the hillside. I could hear nothing but the breeze. I was alone.

Security cameras commanded the slow parting of the gates after closely scrutinising my face. I made my way down the path towards the grand house that was now in full view, travelling under the watchful eyes of crows that lurked amidst the gaunt branches. After eventually reaching the door I pushed the bell. Upon release of my finger it could be heard resonating through the house. There was silence. It seemed like nothing was happening so I went to press it again and just before my outstretched finger reached the button, the door swung open and from the shadows emerged an immaculately presented man with a look of lifelessness impressed on his face.

'Mr Sutcliff, do come in Sir, Dr Alberton has been awaiting your arrival.'

Without as much as a flicker of expression, he asked me to follow him before disappearing into a poorly lit hallway. The sound of his shoes connecting with the hard floor was my only point of reference when he vanished in the patches of darkness where the intermittent wall lamps could not reach. Suddenly, he stopped.

'Here we are Sir.'

He halted across to the right where a light retrieved half of his face from the darkness. On closer inspection, it was a neon sign and in bold letters it read:

'The Gallery'

'Dr Alberton will see you in here Mr Sutcliff. However, I must make you aware that he is running a little late this morning as there has been urgent business for him to attend to.'

I nodded politely.

'There are two chairs at the far side of The Gallery. Please be seated at whichever it is you would like and there is a mineral water on the table which is yours. Enjoy your stay Mr Sutcliff.'

Just as he turned to walk away, I asked, 'Is it okay if I have a look around The Gallery?'

'Oh of course Sir. You don't really have a choice, it's everywhere!'

It was that final comment that drew a wry smile from his face that was so weak that it hardly creased the skin around his eyes. And before I had digested his comment, he was gone.

I peered up at the sign once more. I can't deny that nerves crept in as I considered what awaited me behind it. Eventually, I pushed the door open with the tips of my fingers and the most lurid light overwhelmed my vision immediately. It took a moment of uncomfortable wincing before my eyes readjusted and I slid in through the door that closed behind me.

The room was perfectly square and the walls were bright white, which amplified the intensity of the lighting. But there was something far more disconcerting about my new surroundings. On every wall hung a scattering of pictures which I can say made for uncomfortable viewing. One presented a woman with sorrowful eyes and grotesque lips that had ballooned to a point where they were smeared with black and yellow bruising. Another was a snapshot of a female torso, so emaciated it could hardly be distinguished from a carcass. Her chest however, was made up of two huge breasts that were completely misshapen. That was the theme that ran throughout. Every image presented bodies that were wrapped in fluorescent plastics, Latex and bondage but each one was marred by some hideously unnatural feature. The picture quality and aesthetic presentation were outstanding, but the message was one that echoed in an emotionless hollow. I had to leave. An arrow that hovered above another set of double doors across the room directed my escape. On the other side was an equally bright space where two leather chairs were placed either side of a glass table just as the gentleman had suggested. I went and took a seat.

I wasn't sure how long had passed but my hand began to tremble slightly. The silence created the perfect conditions for my riotous thoughts to fight for my attention. The frantic tapping of my foot followed to accompany my shivering hand. Despite my attempts to fight back the cacophony of parasitic memories, I quickly latched back onto the one that brought me the most discomfort. I was laid back next to her in our bedroom. That window! Does she remember that window? I often think to myself. The one that served as a gateway for the grey light of dawn to pour in and expose us as two imperfect slabs of meat pressed against one another. It was stunning. That window hung like an illustration of a bleak morning against the beige walls of our first home. There was very little inside that house but to me it was filled with dreams of our future; they still play out in my mind to this day as some fictitious dramatisation of what I thought our lives would look like.

'Mr Sutcliff.' Said an assertive voice. The background came into focus.

I peered up at a very slender man resembling a wisp of smoke, so pale and slight that he almost dissolved as he drifted into the room.

'Ah! Dr Alberton! I do apologise, I was daydreaming.'

'Were you daydreaming or day-nightmaring, Mr Sutcliff?' He questioned smugly as he presented his hand for an embrace. I offered no response as we shook. 'And it's Felix. You can drop the Doctor.'

I nodded. 'In that case, it's James.'

'That explains it then. I always have wondered what the J stood for,' he said in a leading tone whilst handing me an iPad.

I inspected the screen and cringed once I realised that it was my own article. It read:

'Mind Control Techniques make Dr Alberton a Modern Day Villain.'

A few seconds passed before I'd decided that I had seen enough so I forcefully flicked the cover over the front of the iPad and placed it back on the table in front of Dr Alberton. He wanted to create the impression that he was willing to reserve judgement so he refrained from speaking, but the smile was more debilitating than any words he could have spoken.

'I particularly like the way you have summarised my new venture as 'mind control techniques;' that one... that really brings it home for me.' He adjusted his small round spectacles to punctuate his point.

'You know those were my words but not my opinions. You do what is expected of you to navigate a path for yourself. Especially in journalism. I don't believe in half the things I wrote Sir... Felix.'

'And isn't that just the problem James? You tarnished my work and my values without a second of consideration. You didn't even consider its impact on you. If you believe that what you do exists in a vacuum, then unfortunately you end up in a vacuum yourself.'
I nodded uncomfortably.

'And that is why I have returned Felix. I am thrashing in a wasteland to try and put things right. I don't know if this will help but it seems necessary. Please, allow me to continue.'

I removed my mobile phone from my top pocket, and under the beady glare of Dr Alberton, I switched on the Dictaphone and placed it cautiously between us. A gentle nod indicated that we were ready.

'How is this new project working out for you James?'

I gave him a stern look to reject his attempts to meander away from the purpose of the discussion. Silence followed but his smile didn't falter.

'You got sacked from the last role, didn't you? Am I correct in saying that? I don't want to misplace the facts here that's all James.'

I tried to sustain my approach but his composed attack had immediately dismantled my resilience.

'Yes! Yes Felix! I got sacked! Why is this important? What do I have to do to reassure you that my intentions are honest?' My display was an effusive one but he did not flinch.

'One more question. Why?'

It quickly became apparent that I was going to have to play his game to get the results that I needed. This realisation forced a deep exhale as I pulled myself together.

'Because I skipped work.'

'Is that all?'

'I did it a lot. I didn't answer their calls. I didn't even look at their emails. They tried to call

Sarah, my girlfriend, but I demanded that she never answered.'

His smile quickly transformed into a practiced look of confusion. 'But where were you that was of such importance?'

I know he knew. His sarcastic tone made my skin crawl so I didn't answer.

'Quite typical of a man with your condition,' he mumbled.

I imagined myself walking out at that point but I couldn't. I proceeded with my interview without prompt as it felt like the only way.

'I walked through The Gallery Felix. I didn't have you down as an artist?'

'I am not. My cognitive makeup defines me ultimately as a man of science but art gives me a sense of the bigger picture. It's good mental practice to see the beauty in what you do.'

'But, pardon me Felix, I struggled to see the beauty in those pictures. Quite the opposite.'

'Of course, but being a 'Plastic Surgeon,' as the laymen will have me titled, it is important to expose the ugly side to take pride in what I do. Art is art. Its function is to be striking or it bears no functionality to the world at all. The real beauty is in the many hundreds of subjects that have left my theatre as a version of themselves that they have always imagined being.'

'So, allow me to cut to the chase. The headline news, the thing that makes people question you the most,' I said whilst removing an old article from my pocket, 'is that 'a Plastic Surgeon has bought the rights to one of the most controversial mind medications in history.' You have claimed that 'this can revert people back to a 'human' state that has been numbed by a benign society where mental wellbeing is a second thought, presenting dangers in a time where technology and illusive power have dislodged our identities.' 'Allow me to reiterate James. The real beauty is in the many hundreds of subjects that have left my theatre as a version of themselves that they have always imagined being. This is very on brand for me and compliments my field of work. What I deal with are the malfunctions of a society where anything organic is being replaced with a homogenous necessity for people to work and live in a confused state. I picture the baron world beyond these hills where masses of faceless people wander in their drones. And they wonder why people are finding less reasons to pull themselves from their beds. It's the condition of our ill-defined generation James.'

I sat and listened to every word scatter like salt in my vulnerable wounds.

'I know why you are here James. Turn off the Dictaphone and ask me for my help.'

His comments had forced me to retreat. My heart gathered pace as those familiar memories crept back in. I always pictured a break up as some big explosive event but ours wasn't. It was a long, underwhelming expiry that ground her perseverance to dust. Sarah, you were the final consequence of the ugly tumour that grew from a careless pursuit of misguided ambitions. I watched your face fade away from my bed bound state but I couldn't express the torture of my affliction. I imagined climbing over your divine body that radiated under the caress of our final dawn and in my dreamy state I stood beside the window, no longer an illustration hanging on the wall, but instead it presented a dreary landscape that consumed the horizon. It was real. The veil of naivety had lifted and I knew that things were not as they had seemed at a simpler time.

'James, we have come too far for me to change the course that has brought us to our state of mental decay. All I can do is a little plastic surgery.'

'You make money from people's misery!' I asserted uncontrollably through gritted teeth.

'And you are trying to make money from me with your news. We are all little pieces of a broken picture.' He smiled and rose from his seat. 'Now, do you want my help or not?'

THE MAN WHO MARRIED A SANDWICH
David Cook

Delectable parma ham. Spicy chorizo. Pepper jack cheese. A sprinkling of red onion. Tangy peppers, hot jalapenos, and a dollop of mayonnaise to cool down the fire. All in a lightly toasted ciabatta. It was the most beautiful sandwich Gary had ever seen. He wasn't sure he could even bring himself to eat it. If he could, he'd marry it.

Why *couldn't* he marry it?

After all, he'd never met a woman he wanted to marry. He considered all the women in his office to be beneath his lofty standards, and he'd been quite happy to voice this opinion to them on a daily basis until HR had got involved. This sandwich, though? It was something else. He definitely couldn't eat it… no, not it – *her*. It would be like taking a bite out of the Mona Lisa. He placed her reverentially in the fridge, clearing the top shelf so she could have it to herself.

And then he thought. He planned. He called a couple of wedding venues in London. He asked questions. He called a few more wedding venues. Money changed bank accounts – quite a lot of money 'because this is rather unusual', as the voice on the other end of the phone had said. A venue was booked. A reverend was hired. It was on.

Before he knew it, the day came. Gary drove himself and his sandwich, which he'd named Teresa (so that they could be nicknamed 'G and T', his old grandma's favourite drink) from their home in Watford to the old reception venue he'd booked in Wimbledon. He sang along to an eighties soft rock radio station. Teresa, now in a portable mini-fridge strapped into the passenger seat, didn't. Gary loved how quiet she was. One of his problems with women was their constant chatter. He appreciated the way Teresa listened to his opinions about that bastard Carl at work, why there's nothing wrong with dog fighting no matter what the do-gooders say, and just what their local supermarket can do with all that gluten-free and organic crap they keep filling their shelves with.

And then they were there. Gary parked next to an old grey building with broken windows and unpleasant graffiti on the walls. It was being knocked down the following day, he'd been told. Not the best of places, he knew, but he'd been unable to secure somewhere more reputable given the 'uniqueness' of his relationship. He unstrapped Teresa and carried her inside. The paint was peeling, the ceiling had fallen down in one corner and the air smelled faintly of urine. Still, Gary didn't mind and Teresa didn't make her feelings known one way or the other.

They met the Reverend, a stooping little chap with a bristly moustache called Mike. Gary thought naming your moustache was a bit weird, but as a man about to marry a sandwich he didn't feel like he could really comment. Other than that he got on well with the Reverend Percy Fishguts. ('Pronounced 'feeshgootz'', he'd told them. 'My grandfather was Latvian.'). The Reverend did the ceremony, having dragged a couple of bewildered Japanese tourists, who'd got lost on their way to the tennis, in from the street to act as witnesses. Then he announced, 'You may kiss your wife!'

After three or four minutes of awkwardness, the Reverend and the tourists left Gary and Teresa to it and went outside to enjoy the sunshine. Eventually, Gary surfaced, smelling of aging meat and bread. In his passion, he'd nibbled off a bit of Teresa's ham. Still, she didn't seem bothered. Then he realised he'd forgotten to hire a photographer, so he took a quick wedding selfie of them both and uploaded it to Facebook for his mum to see. She'd refused to come ('What do you mean,

you're marrying a *sandwich*? Are you *insane*?'),
so he wanted to rub her nose in it a little.

He hadn't been able to afford a honeymoon,
but he and Teresa did enjoy a quick trip into the
city for a whirl on the London Eye before they
headed home to consummate the marriage.

Six months later, life wasn't going so well. Gary
had put Teresa in her mini-fridge, and placed
the fridge on his second-favourite armchair. He
kept the door open so they could watch repeats
of Bullseye together – his favourite ever show –
but no matter what he did, she wasn't happy.
She didn't like that he put tomato sauce on all
his meals, even Coco Pops. She didn't like that
he only changed his underpants once a week.
She didn't like his drinking. Okay, she
never *said* any of this, but he could feel the
disapproval radiating from her crusts. The
atmosphere was becoming distinctly chilly –
and not because of the fridge. He started to stay
out late after work.

Then one night, Gary came home later than
ever. He was several dozen sheets to a
hurricane. He had crumbs dotted around his
mouth. His breath smelled of cured bacon,
smoked turkey, Swiss cheese and ranch
dressing. As he stumbled into the lounge, he
fancied that Teresa gave him an accusing look.

'What are you staring at?' he roared. He'd finally had enough. 'What, you think I've been with another... another sandwich? Is that what you think? Well, yes, fine, yes I bloody have! You sit there, day in, day out, giving me that look, nothing I do is ever good enough for you! And look at you! You're getting old, there's mould round your edges, your mayo is starting to turn, and what the hell does your ham look like? And you're starting to stink! Is it any wonder I've finally turned to younger, tastier sandwiches?! It's a wonder it's taken me this long!'

He moved closer to Teresa, and began to bellow at wherever her face would be if she were a person and not, in fact, a sandwich. 'You know what? I'm sick of you! I wish I'd never married you! You're a... what's it called, a... a millstone around my neck! All my friends go to Subway every night, they're getting hot, tasty foot-longs filled with salami and chicken and beef and toasted cheese... and I have to come home to *you*, you stale old hag!'

Their neighbours heard the bellowing continue until well into the early hours before it, rather suddenly, stopped.

A few days later, the police kicked the door in. They'd been called by the postman, who'd glanced in the window and been alarmed at what he'd seen.

Two uniformed officers marched into the lounge and surveyed the scene. On one armchair was a small fridge, its door lolling open. A half-rotten sandwich filled with rancid meat was inside. On the floor lay Gary, surrounded by blood. His tongue hung from his mouth and eyes stared blankly at the ceiling. Between his ribs was a kitchen knife.

The police ruled it as murder, but never did find the killer. They didn't pay much attention to the ciabatta crumbs next to Gary's corpse, or the blob of mayo on the knife handle.

Contributors

Abigail Brookes is a third year student at Manchester Metropolitan University, studying English Literature with History, with a passion and desire to pursue a career in the publishing industry as a copy-editor. Abigail has an interest in the complexities surrounding the representation and interpretation of literature and art, specifically in satire and gothic fiction.

Ayesha Kinley is a third year English student at MMU. Ayesha hopes to pursue a career in the publishing industry as a copy editor. Influenced by studies in Critical and Cultural Theory, Ayesha has an interest in both considering how art mediates our understanding of the world and how art can express subjects that otherwise are disregarded.

Andrew Ballantyne has always been interested in the impact that society has on individuals. Whilst at University, he studied Sociology and his dissertation looked at the way in which 21st century life affects body image, self-perception and mental well-being. It wasn't until he quit his corporate job after 3 years that he started to revisit some of these ideas with a new perspective, developed by his experiences in an environment characterised by financial progression. 'Plastic' is Andrew's first notable attempt to connect his collection of thoughts, opinions and experiences, all of which combine to communicate a particular message in the story.

David Cook's stories have been published in a number of places, including *Flash Fiction Magazine*, *Spelk* and *Sick Lit Magazine*, who nominated him for the Pushcart Prize. He also featured in *A Box of Stars Beneath the Bed: The 2016 National Flash Fiction Anthology*. Follow him on Twitter: @davidcook100.
www.davewritesfiction.wordpress.com,.

He lives in Bridgend, Wales, with his wife, daughter and cats.

Thomas McColl lives in London and has had short stories and poems published in *Bare Fiction*, *Iota*, *Envoi*, *Prole*, *International Times* and *Smoke: A London Peculiar* and in anthologies by Hearing Eye, Eyewear and Shoestring Press. His first full collection of flash fiction and poetry, *Being With Me Will Help You Learn*, is available now from Listen Softly London Press.

Nick Ryle Wright is a writer of short fiction, originally from Southampton but now based in the New Forest. He has had stories published in The Nottingham Review, Paper and Ink Zine, Rockland, Open Pen (online), Firewords and Flight Journal. He has recently started reading for The Nottingham Review and can be found on Twitter @nickrylew.

Ian Seed's short story *Italian Lessons* (2017) is published by Like This Press. He has two collections of short-short fiction and prose poems, *Identity Papers* (2016) and *Makers of Empty Dreams* (2014), both from Shearsman. He teaches at the University of Chester.

Lauren Dugan is an artist whose work reflects ideas about man's relationship with technology turning sour, basing drawings on hyper-realistic Japanese robotics and human sized doll parts. Playing on ideas of the concept of 'Black Noise' being an empty space that we cannot see, only accessible through radio transmissions and advanced technology. We can speak to ghosts trapped in the abyss.

Lauren is a third year Illustration with Animation student at Manchester Metropolitan University, with a desire to create bold, narrative pieces reflecting on gothic art movements, uncomfortable melancholy themes and the uncanny valley.

Josh Harrison is a third year Illustration & Animation student from Manchester School of Art, with an interest in human relationships, be them interpersonal or on a larger scale but particularly our interactions with an increasingly image based culture, where context is key. Work is often produced in mixed media, predominantly through collage, print and mark-making. Inspired by the irreverent work of Dada Photomontage artists including Hannah Höch and Kurt Schwitters through to current practising collagist such as John Stezaker.

The Black Noise pieces are centred around our increasingly strained and important relationship with the natural world.

Erkembode is a multidisciplinary Mimih artist based in Leeds. His art has variously been described as irreverent, outsider, spiritual, modernist, cutesy, not art, crude, prolific, pointless, phallic, beat, cheap, childlike, responsive, mischievous, non-academic, difficult, purposeful, instinctual. He runs Bear Press, makes films with A616 mate Josh Alexander and sound with PiLGRiMiMiH Ben Morris & Siân Williams.

Erkembode.weebly.com

A reed stylus pressed onto wet clay. Revered in museums, beautiful. Dot-matrix, inkjet, laser, thermal. Receipts. A mountain of receipts. Sainsbury's are my favourite. Yorkshire Bank second. Mega Value third. Spirits that project themselves onto walls, mischievous and x-ray. Paper thin, living in the cracks. Their country is dreaming. Mimih. When people talk about Receipt Mimih, first they don't talk about art or poetry, they compare prices and supermarkets and bank balances. Receipts are material, image, a text; Mimih fold time.

Roselyn Edwards an illustrator animator from Liverpool currently living in Manchester and studying at Manchester school of art. With Animation being her main study she focuses on the idea of lost or untold stories, folklore and peoples history. In her illustration work she uses lino cuttings to create patterns with limited colours. Whilst in her animation work she uses stop motion animation and back light paper cuttings, to create a silhouetted style.

The inspiration for her work comes from the city of Manchester and the use of the Manchester Worker Bee, something that is seen all over the city and is used to symbolise the work ethic of the city and the hub of activity that Manchester is meant to be – something that it fails to be to the homeless of this city.

Homelessness in the heart of Manchester is something which is often overlooked. Homeless people are everywhere yet they are no longer considered people, they fade into the background of the city and cease to be noticed; becoming part of the scenery. They are the Black Noise of the city, the thing we pass every day and no longer think of.